SASQUATCH FOR
SUZAN LINKO
HUCKLEBERRY FOREST
SMILE
BONES
COAL BEAR
HURL GLAK
LINK FALLING
TRUNKS

A SMILE FOR SASQUATCH

A MISSING LINK STORY

BY STEVEN MARTEN

ILLUSTRATED BY
AARON CUSHLEY

INSIGHT
KIDS

San Rafael, California

Sasquatch smiled as he put the last dab of color on his welcome mat. Thatched from grass and colored with berries, it was the perfect invitation to friends, he thought. Then again, how could he know? He'd never had a friend before.

Sure, there were those boys from Big Horn.

And that balloonist from Gilhooley.

There was also that shaman from Sourdough, but he was a cheater.

Sasquatch placed the mat outside his cave and stood back to admire its beauty. It even had the Sasquatchian phrase for *welcome*, splotched right there in huckleberry juice.

"Hurlglak," he crooned, enjoying the tickle on his tonsils. And then it was time for his bath. After all, it had been two weeks.

Sasquatch had no sooner turned to pick up his scrubby when he heard it—a tinkling on the wind. No, not a tinkling. A *clattering*. Like a cabinet of kitchenware.

He hurried off to investigate.

It was a woman. She had shovels that jangled, sifters that spangled, and a spray of hair as yellow as the sunlight.

"Oh dear," she said, spying Sasquatch. "I hope my clanking didn't disturb you."

Sasquatch stared at her. She shimmered when she moved, and her words came tumbling out of her mouth like a mountain spring. "Yep, I've got my pans and pickaxes with me today. I'm a prospector. That means I look for gold. 'Course, I don't know what I'd do if I ever found any!"

Sasquatch smiled when she smiled, but he wasn't sure why. He just knew how nice it felt.

"Forgive me," she said, wading closer and extending her hand. "My name's Susan. Hello!"

Sasquatch didn't know any fancy words like "hello"— or even what a handshake was—but it was the first time these things had ever happened to him, and for this he was overjoyed. He handed her a huckleberry.

"Why, it's perfect!" she glistened. "Thank you!"

Sasquatch watched as the woman found a spot to work along
a pebbly sandbar. Every now and then she would look up and see
him standing on the shore. "Hello again!" she'd call out. Then he'd
disappear into the woods and return with a huckleberry.

This went on for an entire day: a hello for a huckleberry, and a
huckleberry for a hello. It was their game and Sasquatch loved it.

Some afternoons they would sit under the shade of a tall redwood
as she captivated him with stories of the world beyond the mountains.

One night, Sasquatch fell asleep hoping his new
friend would find all the gold she was looking for.
Mostly, though, he hoped she would stay.

The next day, Sasquatch awoke to find the woman on a mountain ridge, bags packed and moving on. "Goodbye," she shouted, hailing a wave. Sasquatch clambered onto a rock to shout back. He thought *hurlglak*, and then *hello*, but by the time the sounds even reached his throat, she was gone. "Meeaaaaugh!" he groaned sadly.

Sasquatch trudged back to his cave to make some breakfast—though he didn't really feel like eating. He kept staring at an ancient painting on his wall, left from a time when humans and sasquatches lived side by side in these woods. Or at least tried to.

"If only they used the same words," he thought.

The next day, Sasquatch took a deep breath of
mountain air, spat out a fly, and concocted a plan.
It was time for his own prospecting mission . . .
to find words!

The first ones he found were on a sign:
FALLING ROCK. He tested them on his
tongue and discovered that they even
sounded like a boulder rolling down
a hill. He plucked them from their
stem and dropped them in his
bag—the perfect start to his
collection!

Outside a small mining town, he found several more words just ripe for picking. He tested each one, chose his favorites, and added them to his collection.

His next find was more of a challenge.
HOT BATH, it said. 10 CENTS. He wrestled
it from the side of a building and smiled at
the cowboy inside.

"Hel-hello," Sasquatch said in his very best
people voice. "Hot bath, peas?" He waited for the
man to reply, but as eager as he was to have his
first conversation, the timing wasn't right.

Arriving at a narrow mountain pass, Sasquatch sat down to review the day's finds. A carriage approached with children inside, so he waved, smiled, and crooned a few words he thought they'd like. This time the reply was prompt.

AUUUUGH!

SASQUATCH!

The carriage veered, sending a trunk toppling to the ground. Sasquatch gathered it up, clapped it closed, and raced after them. He had no words for, "Wait, I have your trunk!" so he shouted something like

Potato! Just then, Sasquatch's foot hit a fallen rock, and he went tumbling over an embankment, falling **down, down, down** into Old Kemp Creek.

Sasquatch had never been in this part of the
creek before, and he had never seen anything like
what lay before him now: an abandoned wreckage,
half covered in vines and wedged into the hillside,
looking as if it had been there a long time.

He approached cautiously. There was nothing
left of the driver except his bones and a few front
teeth, just enough for a strange smile.

Sasquatch stepped back, rubbed his hands together, and cracked open the carriage like a giant walnut. *Floosh!* Pouring over his feet were hundreds of small, slab-shaped objects smelling of leather and old trees. He sniffed one and carefully opened it with his thumbs. He looked closer. *Could it be?*

WORDS!
Millions of them!

Sasquatch gathered the books, the trunk, and most of
the driver, and carried them to the water's edge where he
headed downstream toward his cave.

He felt like he was high on a mountaintop, but it was
really just Old Kemp Creek.

With no limit to the words he was learning, Sasquatch could talk
about anything now. And his new houseguest, "Bones," was the best
listener he'd ever met.

"Listen to this!" he said, opening a book called *Treasure Island*.

"I saw a figure leap with great rapidity behind the trunk of a pine.
What it was, whether bear or man or monkey, I could in no wise tell."

"Can you imagine seeing something like that?" he asked. Bones
slouched, then fell to the floor losing two more teeth.

Sasquatch reattached them with some tape from the trunk and said
softly, "Well, I can't."

He smiled at Bones . . . but the smile slowly faded.

Sasquatch stared for a long time at his guest with the missing teeth, the
dress, and the hay for hair . . . and then bowed his head. "I think I owe you
an apology. I think I wanted you to be something you're not."

Sasquatch gazed again at the painting on his wall. He lay awake wondering if he was wrong about all this word business. Maybe what he yearned for was to run and grunt and play with other sasquatches, free to be exactly as he was. "Hurlglak," he whispered softly.

Halfway around the world, at that very moment, someone else lay awake. It was Sir Lionel Frost, the infamous adventurer. From the glaciers of Antarctica to the deserts of Africa, Sir Lionel had seen—and almost photographed—some of the rarest beasts on Earth. Tonight, he was recording his greatest hope in the pages of his journal.

"The sasquatch," Sir Lionel scribed, "that wondrous missing link between man and beast, and a fellow I should only be lucky enough to meet someday."

He looked across to the dodo sitting on his desk. "And why shouldn't I be so lucky?" he boasted. "I am Sir Lionel Frost!"

With sleep hard to come by, Sasquatch rifled through the trunk outside, unwrapping a lantern. As the light grew, something in the newspaper caught his eye.

"Of course I exist!" retorted Sasquatch. He kept reading. In the article, Sir Lionel spoke of great and monstrous pursuits, high adventure, and a place where maybe—*just maybe*—sasquatches still roamed the earth.

"There . . . *that's* where I belong!"

He rummaged through his stacks of books until he found just the title he was looking for: *Magnificent Ships and How to Build Them*! He carried it out to the creek, taking the lantern and his houseguest with him.

"I'm traveling to London to find Sir Lionel Frost," he told Bones, "and I'm going to need your help!"

Together they worked through the night, crafting the magnificent ship. By dawn, she was complete and ready for her maiden voyage.

He pushed the vessel into the creek and lifted Bones onto
the part where it looked like someone could sit. Sasquatch had
never really seen a ship before, and he immediately wished his
book had more pictures.

She sat oddly on the water for a second, before tilting and
collapsing in a heap. "Not what I hoped for," he grumbled as
he watched Bones slide off into the flow of water and drift
around the bend. Gone.

"I've got to get to Sir Lionel," he sputtered.

"Or," he reconsidered, "get Sir Lionel to come to me!"

Sasquatch retreated to his cave as fast as he could. With a pen and ink, he wrote his first correspondence: an invitation to Sir Lionel Frost to come to Old Kemp Creek and meet a real sasquatch!

"He *has* to come," Sasquatch thought as he sealed the letter. Then, under the cover of darkness, he crept into the mining town to send it off.

At the post office, Sasquatch dropped the letter into the mail slot and waited for Sir Lionel. Then he waited some more.

The waiting tied his belly in knots, so he nervously flipped through a newspaper. Splashed across the front page were photos of Sir Lionel in his study alongside skeletons and stuffed animals. Sasquatch began to pace, wearing down the floor.

"Wait a minute!" he thought, "What am I doing here? I just invited a man who pursues mythic beasts! And did I ever ask why he *does* that?" Sasquatch could only come up with one reason a man would have skeletons in his house. They were his trophies!

THE DAILY GAZETTE

THE DAILY GAZETTE

ECCENTRIC EXPLORER'S COLLECTION SNUBBED BY SCIENTIFIC COMMUNITY

Sasquatch had to retrieve that letter . . .
but how? Best he could tell, there was only
one way to get inside that locked post office.
Sasquatch squeezed his enormous body into
the post office window. "I'm in!" he declared.

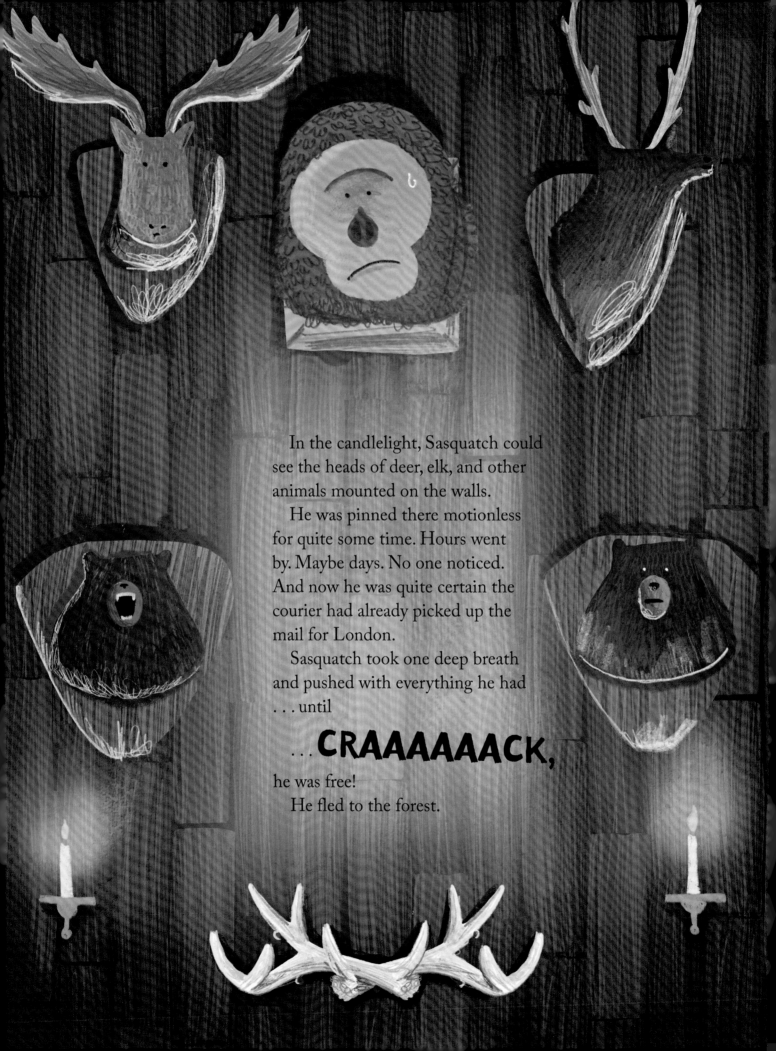

In the candlelight, Sasquatch could see the heads of deer, elk, and other animals mounted on the walls.

He was pinned there motionless for quite some time. Hours went by. Maybe days. No one noticed. And now he was quite certain the courier had already picked up the mail for London.

Sasquatch took one deep breath and pushed with everything he had . . . until

. . . **CRAAAAAACK,**

he was free!

He fled to the forest.

Sasquatch's mind raced like his feet. Maybe he couldn't stop
Sir Lionel from coming, but he *could* get away. He'd done that
his whole life. If he could make it to Old Kemp Creek he would
keep on running. He would run, he would swim, and he would
find a new cave where he could be safe, just like bef—

"PLEASE! WAIT!"

Sasquatch stopped. He stood
very still. The unfamiliar voice
had come from somewhere
behind him.

It sounded a bit like
Susan's . . . only elegant
and more worldly. In that
moment, the letter he had
worked so hard to retrieve
flitted from the brush like a
butterfly, tumbled over the breeze,
and placed itself within his grasp.

"Hm," he smiled. "I got it back!"

He turned around slowly to see Sir
Lionel Frost smiling, in awe, back at him.

"Sir Lionel Frost, I presume? Hello!"

"I don't believe it! You can speak?"

"Yes. And um, I write as well," Sasquatch said
with a chuckle, wishing he had a huckleberry.

Sasquatch watched as Sir Lionel took that first confident step toward him. He imagined the many stories they would tell and the adventures they would seek. He could feel the words come bubbling up into his throat—they had so much to talk about.

INSIGHT
KIDS

An Imprint of Insight Editions
PO Box 3088
San Rafael, CA 94912
www.insighteditions.com

■ Find us on Facebook: www.facebook.com/InsightEditions
🐦 Follow us on Twitter: @insighteditions

Published by Insight Editions, San Rafael, California, in 2019.

Library of Congress Cataloging-in-Publication Data available.

ISBN: 978-1-68383-700-8

Publisher: Raoul Goff

Associate Publisher: Vanessa Lopez

VP Children's Publishing and Business Development:
Elaine Piechowski

Creative Director: Chrissy Kwasnik

Senior Designer: Stuart Smith

Senior Production Editor: Elaine Ou

Senior Production Manager: Greg Steffen

Insight Kids would like to thank Chris Butler, Arianne Sutner,
Martin Pelham, Madeline Hampton, and Jessica Pearson for their
collaboration and creativity.

ROOTS of PEACE ⊕ REPLANTED PAPER

Insight Editions, in association with Roots of Peace, will plant two
trees for each tree used in the manufacturing of this book. Roots
of Peace is an internationally renowned humanitarian organization
dedicated to eradicating land mines worldwide and converting
war-torn lands into productive farms and wildlife habitats. Roots
of Peace will plant two million fruit and nut trees in Afghanistan
and provide farmers there with the skills and support necessary for
sustainable land use.

Manufactured in China by Insight Editions

10 9 8 7 6 5 4 3 2 1

STEVEN MARTEN

Dad of two small boys and married to a teacher of creative
writing, Marten has spent sixteen years in the world of
story. He has written a trilogy of graphic novels recently
acquired by Glenát Editions, adapted *Cloudy with a Chance
of Meatball*s for video game platforms, and contributed to
story development and dialogue for the *VeggieTales* series.
The Martens currently reside in Nashville.

AARON CUSHLEY

Aaron Cushley is an illustrator from Belfast with a passion
for animals and drawing. "I let my inner child loose, and I
gave him a pencil."

Dear Sir Lionel Frost

As famed seeker of mythical beasts You may be interested in this Proposition. I can reveal to you the as yet undiscovered creature, known as the Sasquatch. Follow the trail along old Kempo Creek in ~~the two~~ Washington State and You will find him.

I am truly the reel deal and I believe You are too

SASQUATCH HUR
SUZAN LINKO FOREST
HUCKLEBERRY
SMILE REST
BONES
COAL
HURL GLAK
LINK FALLING
TRUNKS